W9-BSM-464

HARFORD DAY SCHOOL
715 MOORES MILL RD.
BEL AIR, MD 21014

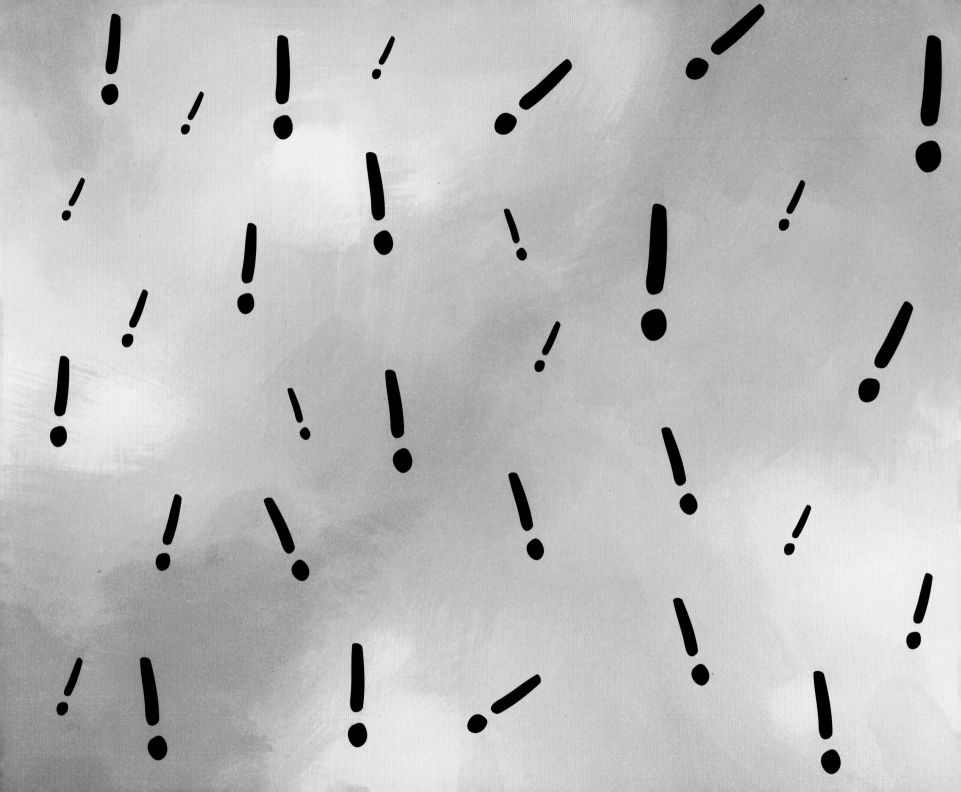

PETER CATALANOTTO PRESENTS . . .

Question Boy

MEETS

Little Miss Know-It-All

A RICHARD JACKSON BOOK

ATHENEUM BOOKS FOR YOUNG READERS • NEW YORK   LONDON   TORONTO   SYDNEY   NEW DELHI

For Lena

Thanks to Scott and Sarah, the staff at Kingwood E.S.,
Barbara, Robin, Linda, and especially Remi and Timmy.

ATHENEUM BOOKS FOR YOUNG READERS · An imprint of Simon & Schuster Children's Publishing Division · 1230 Avenue of the Americas, New York, New York 10020 · Copyright © 2012 by Peter Catalanotto · All rights reserved, including the right of reproduction in whole or in part in any form. · ATHENEUM BOOKS FOR YOUNG READERS is a registered trademark of Simon & Schuster, Inc. · For information about special discounts for bulk purchases, please contact Simon & Schuster Special Sales at 1-866-506-1949 or business@ simonandschuster.com. · The Simon & Schuster Speakers Bureau can bring authors to your live event. For more information or to book an event, contact the Simon & Schuster Speakers Bureau at 1-866-248-3049 or visit our website at www.simonspeakers.com. · Book design by Lauren Rille · The text for this book is set in CC Yada Yada Yada. · The illustrations for this book are rendered in watercolor. · Manufactured in China · 1111 SCP · First Edition · 10 9 8 7 6 5 4 3 2 1 · Library of Congress Cataloging-in-Publication Data · Catalanotto, Peter. · Question Boy meets Little Miss Know-It-All / Peter Catalanotto. — 1st ed. · p. cm. · "A Richard Jackson Book." · Summary: A curious boy with non-stop questions meets a girl who seems to know all the answers. · ISBN 978-1-4424-0670-4 · [1. Curiosity—Fiction. 2. Humorous stories.] I. Title. · PZ7.C26878Qu 2012 · [E]—dc22 · 2011000496

HE was Question Boy, squinting hard against the rising sun. His boots scraped the ground. His cape fluttered in the breeze.

On Main Street, Garbage Man was busy freeing the city of filth and rubbish.

"How much stuff can you fit in your truck?" Question Boy asked.

"A lot," Garbage Man answered.

"More than an elephant?"

"Probably," said Garbage Man. "I think so."

"Could you fit a whale in there?"

Garbage Man looked around. Oil Man was turning onto Main Street.

"How about a brontosaurus?"

Garbage Man slowly backed away.

"The moon? Could you fit the whole moon in there?"

Garbage Man jumped into his truck and sped off.

Down the street, Oil Man was saving a family from cold showers.

"What are you doing?" Question Boy asked.

"I'm filling a tank with oil so the people who live here will have hot water and heat when they need it."

"Can I see the tank?"

"There, my work here is finished," Oil Man said. "What? No, you can't see the tank. It's in the basement. Even I've never seen it."

"How do you know it's there? What if someone took the tank for a drive?"

"Ah!" Oil Man said. "It's not an army tank!"

"How do you know if you've never seen it?"
Question Boy asked.

"Well . . . because . . ."

"What if they took the tank out for a drive and you
just filled their whole basement with oil?"

"You can't drive an oil tank!" Oil Man said firmly.

"What's that giant container on your truck?"
Question Boy asked.

Oil Man flinched. "It's . . . a . . . tank. . . ."

"What's in it?" Question Boy asked.

Oil Man stumbled backward. He jumped in his
truck and hurried away.

All day long, Question Boy wandered and wondered. He perplexed Police Woman and panicked Mechanic Man.

He left Wonder Waitress woozy. Even Mailman and Paperboy were no match for his need to know.

No one had enough answers for Question Boy. Sighing, he plopped down in the park. Near his foot, a coin caught his eye. He picked it up. Was it a dime or a nickel?

A voice behind him said, "There are one hundred and eighteen ridges on every dime."

Question Boy turned. "Who are you?"

"*SHE* is Little Miss Know-It-All!" Delivery Man yelled as he rode by on his Super Cycle.

"Why are you wearing a crown?"

"It's a tiara. It sparkles *and* holds my hair perfectly in place."

"How many hairs are on your head?"

"Fourteen thousand, one hundred and ninety-six."

Question Boy blinked three times. He held up his coin. "What can I buy with this?"

"Candy, rubber bands, or paper clips."

"How much candy?" he asked.

"Depends on what kind of candy you want."

"What if I want chocolate?"

"Chocolate comes from cacao trees that grow in the Amazon," said Little Miss Know-It-All.

Question Boy wrinkled his nose and scratched his head. "Where does gum come from?" he asked.

"Ancient Greece," she answered.

"What kind of grease?" he asked. "Bacon grease? Car grease?
How old does grease have to be until it turns into gum?"

A crowd began to gather.

"Greece is a country," she said. "Hercules was from Greece!"

"What kind of gum did Hercules chew?" Question Boy asked.

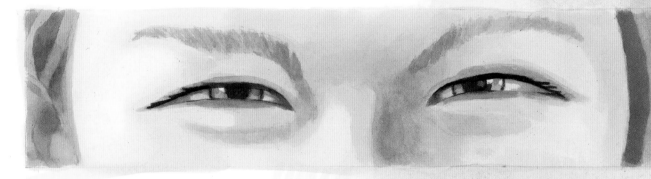

Little Miss Know-It-All narrowed her eyes. Her nostrils
twitched. "Peppermint."

Question Boy whooped! But before he could ask anything
else, she began:

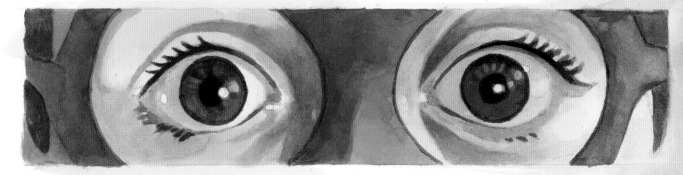

"Cats have thirty-two muscles in each ear!
The Mona Lisa has no eyebrows!
Dolphins sleep with one eye open!
Thomas Edison was afraid of the dark!
A baby camel is called a camelot!
Houseflies hum in the key of F!"

Little Miss Know-It-All never took a breath.

"Kangaroos can't walk backward!
Ketchup was once sold as a medicine!
A giraffe can clean its ears
with its tongue!

Leonardo da Vinci invented pizza!
Hummingbirds can weigh less than a penny!
The first ice cream cones were
rolled-up waffles!

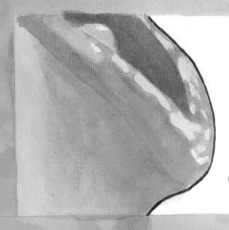

Abraham Lincoln had a
pet turkey named Jack!
Most yawns last six seconds!
Octopuses have three hearts!"

Question Boy's head started to hurt.

"It's against the law to enter or leave Minnesota with a duck on your head! A group of jellyfish is called a smack! Fingernails grow four times faster than toenails! A billion times a million is a brazillian!"

Question Boy sprawled backward. He ducked under his cape.

"ENOUGH!" Police Woman yelled.

But Little Miss Know-It-All went on:

"Hippos run faster than people!

Hamsters blink only one eye at a time!

Benjamin Franklin discovered the electric guitar! Butterflies taste food with their feet! Some turtles can breathe through their rear ends!

A mongoose doesn't look like a goose, it looks more like a meerkat, and a meerkat doesn't look like a cat, it looks more like a prairie dog, and a prairie dog doesn't even look like a dog, it looks more like a squirrel!"

Little Miss Know-It-All stopped. She felt dizzy. Below her, Question Boy lay still.

She looked to the sky, sighed, and dropped her chin to her chest. She watched a leaf skitter past. The crowd slowly parted, making a path for her, and she started to head home.

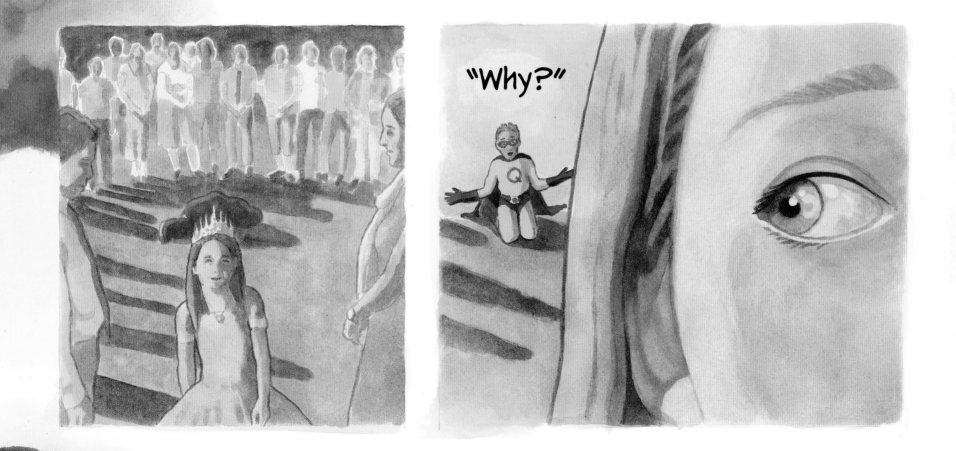

Little Miss Know-It-All froze.

"Why?" Question Boy repeated. "Why can't kangaroos walk backward? Why do octopuses have three hearts? Why do hamsters blink only one eye at a time?" He stood up.

"WHY?"

He heard Little Miss Know-It-All swallow hard.

"Why?" He came closer. "Why?" he asked with every step.

"WHY?"

"Why? Why? Why? Why? Why? Why? Why? Why? Why? Why?"

The crowd gasped.
Little Miss Know-It-All could not take much more.

"Why? Why? Why? Why?
Why? Why? Why? Why?
WHY?"

Question Boy and Little Miss Know-It-All both fell to the ground. Nobody moved.

Somewhere in the distance a dog started barking.
Question Boy watched a cloud shaped like a bunny float by.

Little Miss Know-It-All sat up and straightened her tiara.

"Are you okay?" she asked.

"I think so." Question Boy sat up. "Hey, you asked a question."

"Hey!" she replied. "You didn't."

Little-Miss-Know-It-All stood up and offered her hand.

Question Boy grabbed it and she pulled him to his feet.

"Do you want to come to my house and help feed my turtle?" she asked.

He shrugged. "Sure. I just need to call my mom."

As the sun began to set, Question Boy and Little Miss Know-It-All walked together back up Main Street.

"Can some turtles," he asked, "*really* breathe through their rear ends?"

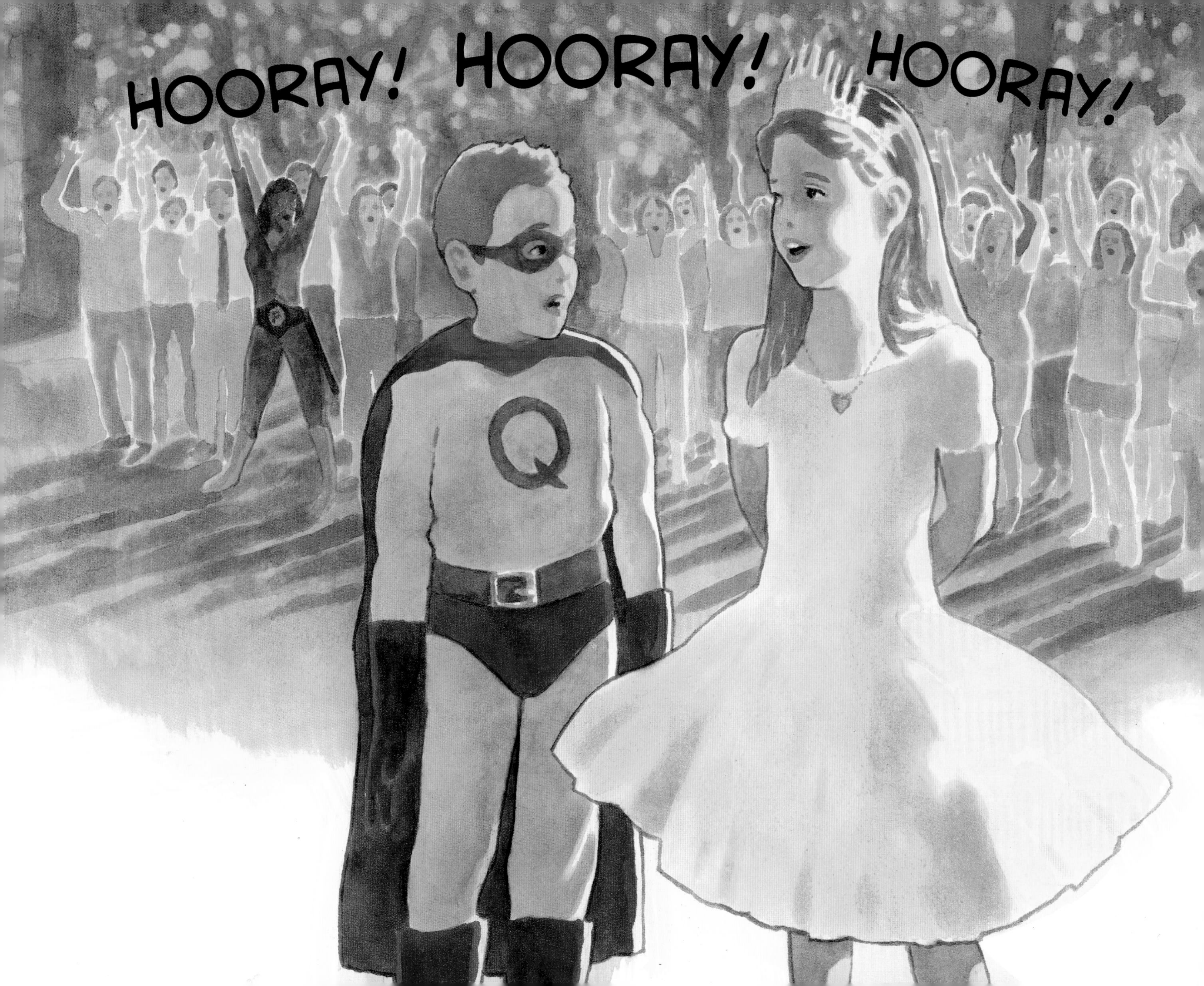
HOORAY!
HOORAY!
HOORAY!

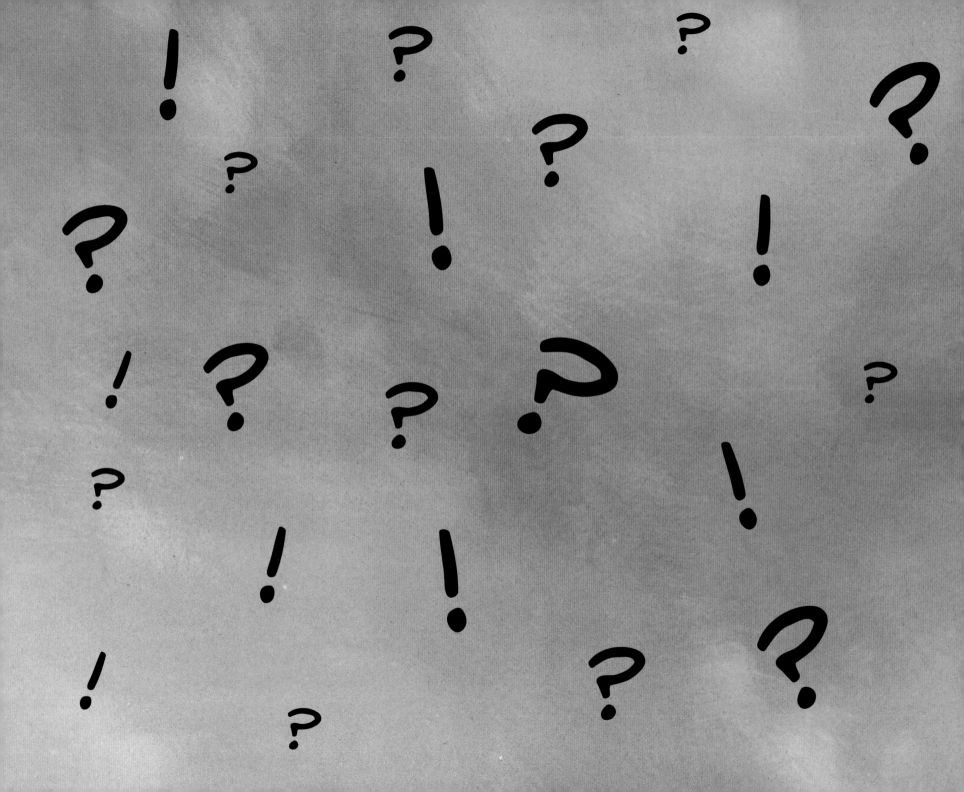